Can you find all of the pictures of the bluebird in this book?
He is hidden throughout this story in eleven different places.
See if you can find them all!

Copyright 2013 by Briley Publishing

All rights reserved

NO PART OF THIS BOOK MAY BE REPRODUCED OR TRANSMITTED IN ANY FORM OR ANY MANNER, ELECTRONIC OR MECHANICAL, INCLUDING PHOTOCOPYING, RECORDING OR BY ANY INFORMATION STORAGE AND RETRIEVAL SYSTEM, WITHOUT PERMISSION IN WRITING FROM THE PUBLISHER

ISBN- 978-0-9860214-3-5 (Hardcover)

Briley Publishing
1690 Briley Rd. Johannesburg, Mi 49751
http://www.facebook.com/TheAdventuresOfLilyAndAva

Dedication Page

The book series The Adventures of Lily and Ava is dedicated to my two daughters Lily and Ryan who are the inspiration behind me writing children's books. I would like to thank all of those who have had a hand in helping me develop my book series, and a special thanks to Crystal Bowan (Editor) and Jim Dombrowski (Illustrator).

To: _____

From: _____

Gordy Briley

THE ADVENTURES OF
Lily & Ava

Sully the Bully

Written by Gordon Briley

Illustrated by Jim Dombrowski

It was early in the spring and the snow was nearly gone.

A few more days and we could play on our lawn.

Ava and I can finally go outside to play,

No need for winter hats or wearing gloves today.

The sun was bright and felt warm on our skin.

Now our springtime adventures were about to begin.

I threw on my shoes and ran out the door,

there were so many things I wanted to explore.

I walked next door and there was Ava on her swing.

"Hey Ava, are you excited that it's spring?"

"I am! I am!" said Ava with glee.

"Lily, you should come to the park with me!"

"You think it's okay? The kids there play rough."

"Ahh Lily, it's no problem, we just have to be tough."

"Yeah, you are right, we make a good team.
They'd better watch out 'cause we're tougher than we seem."

"All right Ava," I said. "To the park we will go!

Maybe there will be some friends that we know."

We rode to the park and we could see kids playing.

We were getting close; could almost hear what they were saying.

I recognized the one kid, his name was Sully.

He was a really big kid and an even bigger bully.

He turned to me and Ava, and then he loudly said,

"Hey, forget the swings and play with me instead."

"We're playing a game that you might like.

It's called, come over here and clean my bike."

Ava yelled out, "That's okay. I don't like to clean.

You're not very nice. I think you're really mean."

"Just kidding, Sully. She doesn't know what she's saying.

We have to go, we can't be staying."

This made him angry and he picked up a stone.

He aimed it at us and yelled, "Go home!"

"Ava, it would be better if we just walked away.

He'll keep picking on us if we stay."

It was too late! Sully grabbed us both by the ear.

He yelled, "Now you two get over here!"

He walked us over to a muddy pit.

"Get in there you two and have a sit."

We sat in the mud which was freezing cold.

"Lily, I really wish I was old."

"I would make him pay for being so mean,

pull his hair and make him scream."

"Ava, that isn't going to help us now,

we're going to have to escape somehow."

"Okay, Lily, let's think of a plan.

We need to escape as soon as we can.

Let's use our imagination to figure this out,

we can beat Sully without a doubt."

"Ava, I know what we can do.

Lean over here so I can whisper it to you."

I told her what to do and where to go.

"You'll have to do it nice and slow."

I quickly yelled, "Hey, Sully, take a look at Steven.

He's getting away, he's probably leaving."

He quickly turned around to check and see,

then Ava slowly crawled behind his knee.

If Sully steps backs he'll trip and fall.

Then we can escape and save us all.

Good old Sully fell for the trick.

He took a step back and began to slip.

He tripped over Ava who was sitting so still,

and into the mud he took a big spill.

It worked perfectly, so we began to run.

We hoped that Sully's bullying was finally done.

Ava looked back and said, "Lily, come on let's go.

Why in the world are you moving so slow?"

"I think that Sully might be hurt.

He's lying face down in the dirt."

"Lily, this is our chance, we have to run.

If he catches us now we are surely done."

We could have run, but it didn't feel right.

If he was hurt he could be there all night.

We slowly walked back and heard a sound.

Sully was crying and hitting the ground.

We grabbed his arm and began to pull,

"Stand up, Sully, here you go."

He came to his knees looking so sad.

"I've treated you terrible, I feel so bad."

"We came back, Sully, because we know you can be good.

Just give it a try, don't you think you should?"

"Thank you both for not running away.

I'm going to be good starting today.

It's time for change, no more being mean.

I'm going to be the best person you have ever seen."

He looked at us and started to smile,

"Could you stay and play a while?"

He reached out his hand for us to shake.

Boy oh boy, what a mistake!

He grabbed us both by the hand,

and back in the mud we did land.

All three of us sat there and had a good laugh.

Now it was time to go home and take a bath.

Sully softly asked, "How can I make up for being so mean?"

We smiled and said, "We have bikes that you can clean."

We all giggled and then said good-bye.

We had helped Sully become a nice guy.

Treating others with kindness is the way to go,

Give it a try and tell everyone you know.

We learned a great lesson and had a blast.

It wasn't our first adventure and certainly not our last!

Want to see the real Lily and Ava?
Go to http://www.facebook.com/TheAdventuresOfLilyAndAva

Please feel free to leave a review. Visit Amazon.com, Goodreads.com, or B&N.com to leave a review.

Thank you and I hope you enjoyed "Sully the Bully."